DANDY THE DIME

MAINLY FOR THE MUFFIN

DANDY THE DIME

Story by **James S. Kerr**

Illustrations by **s. schofer mathews**

Publishers

T. S. DENISON & CO., Inc.

Minneapolis, Minnesota

First Printing—April 1960
Second Printing—May 1961
Third Printing—June 1962
Fourth Printing—September 1964
Fifth Printing—March 1965
Sixth Printing—October 1965
Seventh Printing—June 1966
Eighth Printing—January 1967
Ninth Printing—July 1967
Tenth Printing—January 1968
Eleventh Printing—July 1968
Twelfth Printing—April 1971

Standard Book Number: 513-00317-7
Library of Congress Card Number: 60-10178
Printed in the United States of America
by The Brings Press
Published by T. S. Denison & Company, Inc.
Copyright © 1960 by T. S. Denison & Co., Inc.
Minneapolis, Minn. 55431

DANDY THE DIME

To be so little makes me sad,
I do not look like much.

But I'm big enough to look at
And I'm big enough to touch.

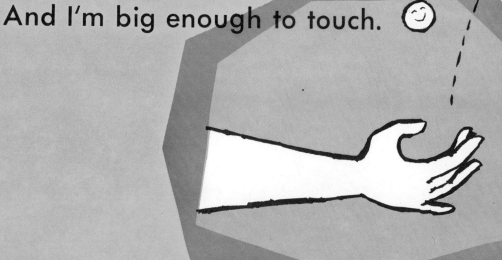

But for so very many things
I cannot meet the cost,
On top of this because I'm small,
Quite easily I'm lost!

A quarter's what I'd like to be,

Or a half-a-dollar piece,

Or a crispy dollar bill,

Then I'd do as I please!

But what's the use of wishing

Or day-dreaming all the time?

All I am and all I'll be

Is just a tiny dime!

My owner thought I wasn't much,
Just a piece of change.

As he walked I'd bounce around
With other coins so strange.
There were quarters and half-dollars
So very big and proud,
But no one heard me jingle, for
The others were so loud.

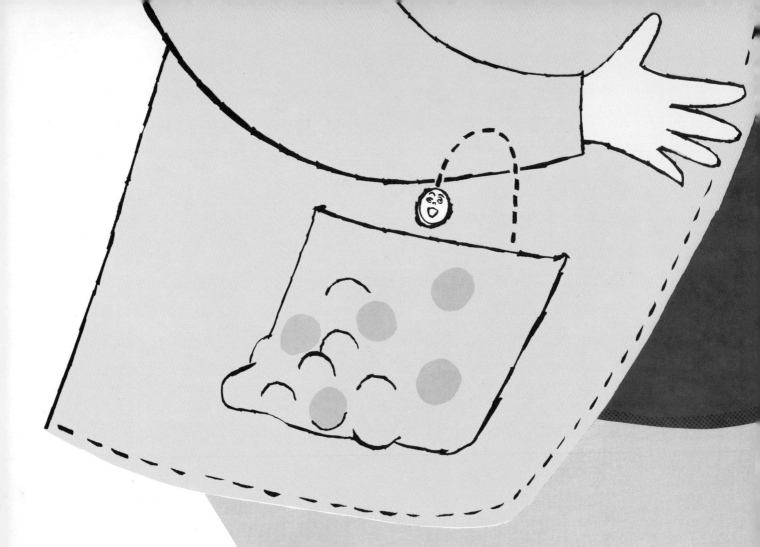

No one heard my jingling,
        And no one needed me.
No one was proud to hold me up
        For all the world to see.
I'd trade my shine to help just once
        Some one, someplace, some time,
Then it wouldn't be so bad
        To be a small thin dime!

My owner had so many coins

His pocket stretched and wore,

And then one day while walking

Finally it tore.

Of course I was the smallest one

And couldn't help but fall,

At first I thought he'd miss me,

But no sir! Not at all!

Ker-plunk! Down to the hard cement,
Then I bounced into the lawn—
My owner never turned around
To notice I was gone!

Between the bright and green grass blades
I rolled and rolled around,

Until I fell flat on my back,
And waited to be found!

And there I slept through all the night
Till drops of morning dew,
Washed away the dust and dirt
And sparkled me like new.
The bright old sun pushed shadows back
And rose up in the sky,
And shone upon me brightly
Till I was warm and dry.

The milkman, in the morning,
Didn't even look my way.

The mailman almost put his foot
Upon me where I lay.
But he was sorting letters,
He didn't have the time
To think or look or stop because
Someone had lost a dime!

A little boy, named Johnny, woke

And saw the lovely day,

He loaded up his toys and things

And headed out to play.

He played he was an Indian Chief

Creeping along the ground . . .

And then, that's right! You guessed!

I knew I would be found!

He picked me up and smiled at me!

He knew what dimes were for!

He ran to ask his mother

If he could go to the store.

"I found a dime," he told her.

"Perhaps I'll buy a toy!"

His mother smiled, and said, "All right!"

"Isn't that just like a boy!"

Johnny held me gently then,
And took me to the store.

And I was proud and happy when
   We two walked through the door.
He looked at all the counters
   Full of many pleasant things,
There was bubble gum, and tiny cars,
   And trucks and secret rings.

Then Johnny asked the store man,

"Which of these things can I buy?"

(I knew there were not many,

But I could not tell him why!)

DIME THINGS

Soda pop, a chocolate bar,

Gum, and candy too,

A tiny toy, and that was it!

He wondered what to do!

He looked and looked and looked again
   To see what he could find,
Until I felt so very small . . .
   I hoped he would not mind
That I was just a little dime
   That could not buy him much.
Just gum and pop and chocolate bars,
   And tiny toys, and such.

I thought I saw a tiny tear
Squeeze into Johnny's eye.
And for a moment I was afraid
That he would start to cry.

But then I knew that everything
    Was going to be all right,
For Johnny turned and left the store—
    And squeezed me very tight!

Well, that was something anyway,

That my new owner thought

That I was more important

Than the things he could have bought!

He took me home without a word

Thinking all the while,

"What to do with just a dime?"

—And then I saw him smile!

I hoped he had the answer

How I could be of use,

(For just because I'm very small

Is really no excuse!)

Then Johnny took me to his room

He dropped me in his bank,

The bank was very empty

And I made a noisy "clank!"

I thought he had forgotten me,
At least it seemed that way.
But at least it was much better
Than if I'd been thrown away!

I was lonely in that little bank—
I must admit it's true,
But then one day I got some friends—
Six pennies bright and new!

Someone, on Johnny's birthday,

Gave him nickels, one, two, three!

And Johnny dropped them in the bank

To keep me company!

He got a shiny nickel for

Running to the store,

He did little jobs for Father

Who gave him several pennies more!

So soon the little bank was full,
Fat and satisfied,
Not room for even one more coin
No matter how he tried.

"It's quite amazing," Father said.
"How fast your savings mount!
"Don't you think it's almost time
You had a bank account?"

"Why yes," said little Johnny,
From his perch atop his stool,
"I think it would be very fine!"

And then that day at school
The teacher told the class the news
That they were going to learn,
How to bank and how to save
The money they could earn!

"How wonderful!" said Johnny.
Then his bank to school he took,
With me and all my fellow coins—

And got his first bank book!

The other children did the same,
Each brought a small amount,

And then they watched their savings grow,
In their **very own** account!

So that is just what happened,
    And it started just with me,
A little dime, so thin and small,
    That no one cared to see.
But Johnny learned that saving
    Will bring him many things—
Much better and much bigger
    Than pop and secret rings!

And me? Well, I'm quite happy
    In the biggest bank in town!
With all my friends for company
    I'll never need to frown!

Now Johnny has his bank account,

A bright new bank book too.

Now Johnny thinks that saving's fun . . .

Don't you?